Gekko Takes Charge

D0180833

Based on the episode
"Terrible Two-Some"

Ready-to-Read

Simon Spotlight
New York London Toronto Sydney New Delhi

SIMON SPOTLIGHT
An imprint of Simon & Schuster Children's Publishing Division
1230 Avenue of the Americas, New York, New York 10020
This Simon Spotlight edition August 2019
Adapted by Ximena Hastings from the series PJ Masks
All rights reserved, including the right of reproduction in whole or in part in any form.
SIMON SPOTLIGHT, READY-TO-READ, and colophon are registered trademarks of Simon & Schuster, Inc.
For information about special discounts for bulk purchases, please contact Simon & Schuster Special Sales at 1-866-506-1949 or business@simonandschuster.com.
Manufactured in the United States of America 0719 LAK
10 9 8 7 6 5 4 3 2 1
ISBN 978-1-5344-5075-2 (hc)
ISBN 978-1-5344-5074-5 (pbk)
ISBN 978-1-5344-5076-9 (eBook)

Greg is playing on his scooter with Amaya and Connor.

"Be careful!" Amaya says.

Greg sighs.

He is tired of being

the youngest.

Then they notice that
everyone is acting
like babies. Oh no!

This is a job for the
PJ Masks!

Amaya becomes Owlette!

Greg becomes Gekko!

Connor becomes Catboy!

They are the PJ Masks!

The PJ Masks search
the city. They find Romeo!

He wants to use
his Baby Beam
to take over the world.

Owlette tries to stop him.

She gets zapped
by the Baby Beam!

Catboy uses his
Super Cat Speed.

He gets zapped too!

"Gasping Gekkos!
My friends are acting
like babies!" Gekko says.

Now he is the oldest
of the PJ Masks!

Gekko takes charge.

He pushes

Romeo's lab away.

The PJ Masks go back
to Headquarters.

Little Owlette and
little Catboy want to play.

"Come on!
You are superheroes, not
two-year-olds!" Gekko says.

Catboy and Owlette start crying.

Being in charge is harder than Gekko thought.

An alarm goes off.

Romeo is on his way!

Gekko has an idea.
They can play and pretend
that they are heroes!

Gekko teaches

little Owlette how to fly.

Then he shows little Catboy how to run fast.

Now they are ready

to fight Romeo!

Romeo arrives with his
Baby Beam.

The PJ Masks work together.

They destroy the Baby Beam!

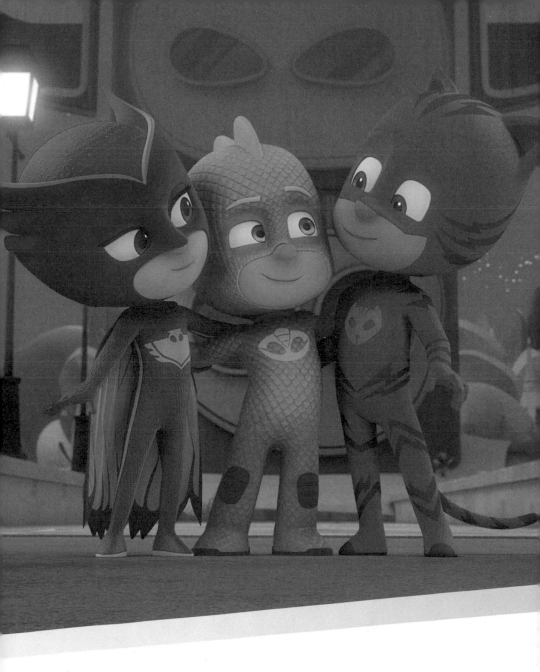

Everyone goes back to
normal.

PJ Masks all shout hooray!

Because in the night,

we saved the day!